Paw Prints

Boxers

by Nadia Higgins

Bullfrog Books

Ideas for Parents and Teachers

Bullfrog Books let children practice reading informational text at the earliest reading levels. Repetition, familiar words, and photo labels support early readers.

Before Reading
- Discuss the cover photo. What does it tell them?
- Look at the picture glossary together. Read and discuss the words.

Read the Book
- "Walk" through the book and look at the photos. Let the child ask questions. Point out the photo labels.
- Read the book to the child, or have him or her read independently.

After Reading
- Prompt the child to think more. Ask: Have you ever seen a boxer? Would you like to play with one?

Bullfrog Books are published by Jump!
5357 Penn Avenue South
Minneapolis, MN 55419
www.jumplibrary.com

Copyright © 2019 Jump! International copyright reserved in all countries. No part of this book may be reproduced in any form without written permission from the publisher.

Library of Congress Cataloging-in-Publication Data

Names: Higgins, Nadia, author.
Title: Boxers / by Nadia Higgins.
Description: Minneapolis, MN : Jump!, Inc., 2018.
Includes index.
Audience: Ages 5 to 8. | Audience: Grades K to 3.
Identifiers: LCCN 2017039653 (print)
LCCN 2017043175 (ebook)
ISBN 9781624967672 (ebook)
ISBN 9781624967665 (hardcover : alk. paper)
Subjects: LCSH: Boxer (Dog breed)—Juvenile literature.
Classification: LCC SF429.B75 (ebook)
LCC SF429.B75 H54 2018 (print) | DDC 636.73—dc23
LC record available at https://lccn.loc.gov/2017039653

Editor: Jenna Trnka
Book Designer: Molly Ballanger

Photo Credits: Jean-Michel Labat/Pantheon/SuperStock, cover; Dora Zett/Shutterstock, 1; Paul Cotney/Shutterstock, 3; Tierfotoagentur/Alamy, 4, 8–9, 23mr; Grigorita Ko/Shutterstock, 5; Stig Karlsson/Dreamstime, 6–7, 23tl; Jody Trappe Photography/Getty, 10–11, 23tr; Susan Schmitz/Shutterstock, 12; Giuseppe Porzani/Adobe Stock, 13 (foreground); Vlue/Shutterstock, 13 (background); Inabella/Shutterstock, 14–15, 23br; Gabriele Maltinti/Shutterstock, 16–17; Helder Almeida/Shutterstock, 18; viafilms/iStock, 19, 23ml; Jennifer Bosvert/Shutterstock, 20–21; Hugo Felix/Shutterstock, 22; justsolove/Shutterstock, 23bl; Csanad Kiss/Shutterstock, 24.

Printed in the United States of America at Corporate Graphics in North Mankato, Minnesota.

Table of Contents

Sweet and Strong	4
A Boxer Up Close	22
Picture Glossary	23
Index	24
To Learn More	24

Sweet and Strong

Look at that dog jump!

It is a boxer.

It has a lot of energy.

Long ago, boxers came from far away.

Where? Germany.

They were bred to work.

They are strong.

muscles ▸

See its muscles?

Boxers like to keep busy. They guard the house. Woof!

cheek

Look at those long cheeks.

Watch out for wet kisses!

Its forehead is wrinkled.
Look at those big eyes.

Time for bed.
Boxers have short noses.
They snore!

Some boxers are tan.
Some are brown.
This one is striped.

Pet one.

Its coat is smooth.

Boxers like to play. Do you want to play with one?

A Boxer Up Close

Picture Glossary

bred
Developed as a dog breed.

guard
Protect.

coat
A dog's fur.

muscles
Body parts that make animals strong and let them move.

Germany
A country in Western Europe.

wrinkled
Folded lines.

Index

cheeks 12
coat 19
energy 5
eyes 15
forehead 15
Germany 6
guard 10
muscles 9
noses 16
play 21
snore 16
work 6

To Learn More

Learning more is as easy as 1, 2, 3.

1) Go to www.factsurfer.com

2) Enter "boxers" into the search box.

3) Click the "Surf" button to see a list of websites.

With factsurfer.com, finding more information is just a click away.